A FUNNY THING HAPPENED AT THE MUSEUM...

For Matyash

—Benjamin

Text copyright © 2017 by Davide Cali.
Illustrations copyright © 2017 by Benjamin Chaud.

Library of Congress Cataloging-in-Publication Data available.

ISBN 978-1-4521-5593-7

Manufactured in China.

Design by Ryan Hayes.
Typeset in 1820 Modern.

10 9 8 7 6 5 4 3 2 1

Chronicle Books LLC
680 Second Street
San Francisco, California 94107

Chronicle Books—we see things differently. Become part of our community at www.chroniclekids.com.

A FUNNY THING HAPPENED AT THE MUSEUM...

Davide Cali   Benjamin Chaud

chronicle books · san francisco

As soon as I walked in, I was charged by a triceratops.

Fortunately, I sought safety among a family of Neanderthals.

To thank them for their help, I entertained them
with my balloon-folding skills.

But then I was chased away by a herd of buffalo.

Suddenly, there was a loud *boom*!

So I ran out of there as fast as I could,
but I accidentally broke something along the way.

I tried my best to put it back together.

Then, I was briefly detained by a lively sculpture.

Thankfully, I was rescued by another one.

After all that action, I decided to catch my breath.

Then I got lost in an unusual stairwell . . .

that led to a secret passage!

It was a real mess
down there.

So I just had to put
things in order.

I really cleaned all over!

And I took care of a few other things, too . . .

I happened to notice that some paintings weren't finished.

I really applied myself.

By then, it was getting late, and I needed to find our class.

I had no problem spotting them . . .

But joining them wasn't as easy . . .

Luckily, I discovered a way to reach them really quickly.

But I probably misunderstood the instructions . . .

and I landed in totally unexplored territory.

Suddenly, I felt far away from everyone.

But that didn't last long.

And THAT is what happened at the museum.

"Well, Henry, it sounds like you had fun after all. Maybe one day you, too, will be an artist."

Who, me? Oh, no . . .
I really don't think so.

Meanwhile . . .

Davide Cali is an author, illustrator, and cartoonist who has published more than 40 books, including *A Funny Thing Happened on the Way to School . . .* , *The Truth About My Unbelievable Summer . . .* , *When An Elephant Falls in Love,* and *I Didn't Do My Homework Because . . .* , which has been translated into 17 languages. He lives in France and Italy.

Benjamin Chaud has illustrated more than 60 books, including *I Didn't Do My Homework Because . . .* , *A Funny Thing Happened on the Way to School . . .* , and *The Truth About My Unbelievable Summer. . . .* He is the author and illustrator of New York Times Notable Book *The Bear's Song, The Bear's Sea Escape, The Bear's Surprise,* and *Farewell Floppy.* He lives in Die, France.